T4-ADO-983

VALENTINE'S DAY

HOLIDAY CELEBRATIONS

Jason Cooper

Rourke
Publishing LLC
Vero Beach, Florida 32964

© 2003 Rourke Publishing LLC

All rights reserved. No part of this book may be reproduced or utilized in any form or by any means, electronic or mechanical including photocopying, recording, or by any information storage and retrieval system without permission in writing from the publisher.

www.rourkepublishing.com

PHOTO CREDITS: Cover, title page, p. 8, 12, 13, 14, 17 © Comstock Images; p. 7 © Brand X Pictures; p. 4, 11, 18, 21 © Lynn M. Stone

Cover: *Friends exchange valentines on February 14, Valentine's Day.*

Editor: Frank Sloan

Cover design by Nicola Stratford

Library of Congress Cataloging-in-Publication Data

Cooper, Jason, 1942-
 Valentine's Day / Jason Cooper
    p. cm. — (Holiday celebrations)
Contents: Valentine's Day — Valentine's cards — Old-fashioned valentines — Valentine symbols — Red and white — Roses are red — Cupid — Romans and Greeks — The first Valentine's Day — Early Valentine's Days.
Includes bibliographical references and index.
 ISBN 1-58952-222-2 (hardcover)
1. Valentine's Day—Juvenile literature. [1. Valentine's Day. 2. Holidays.] I. Title. II. Holiday celebrations (Vero Beach, Fla.)
GT4925 .C66 2002
394.2618—dc21   2002002498

Printed in the USA

CG/CG

TABLE OF CONTENTS

Valentine's Day	5
Valentine Cards	6
Old-fashioned Valentines	9
Valentine Symbols	11
Red and White	13
Roses Are Red	14
Cupid	16
Romans and Greeks	19
The First Valentine's Days	20
Early Valentine's Days	22
Glossary	23
Index	24
Further Reading/Websites to Visit	24

RULES FOR GOOD LISTENING
EYES are watching
EARS are listening
Eyes on Speaker
2. Lips Closed
I LOVE YOU
Have a Happy Day!
All My Love

VALENTINE'S DAY

Valentine's Day is a day for warm thoughts, greetings, and gifts. It is celebrated each February 14.

Valentine's Day is most popular in the United States, Canada, and England. It is sometimes called St. Valentine's Day.

Schoolchildren make valentines for their friends.

VALENTINE CARDS

People send greeting cards called valentines on this day. People send valentines to those for whom they have a special **fondness**. Many valentines say "Be my Valentine" or "I Love You."

A Valentine's Day card made by hand is a treasure to keep.

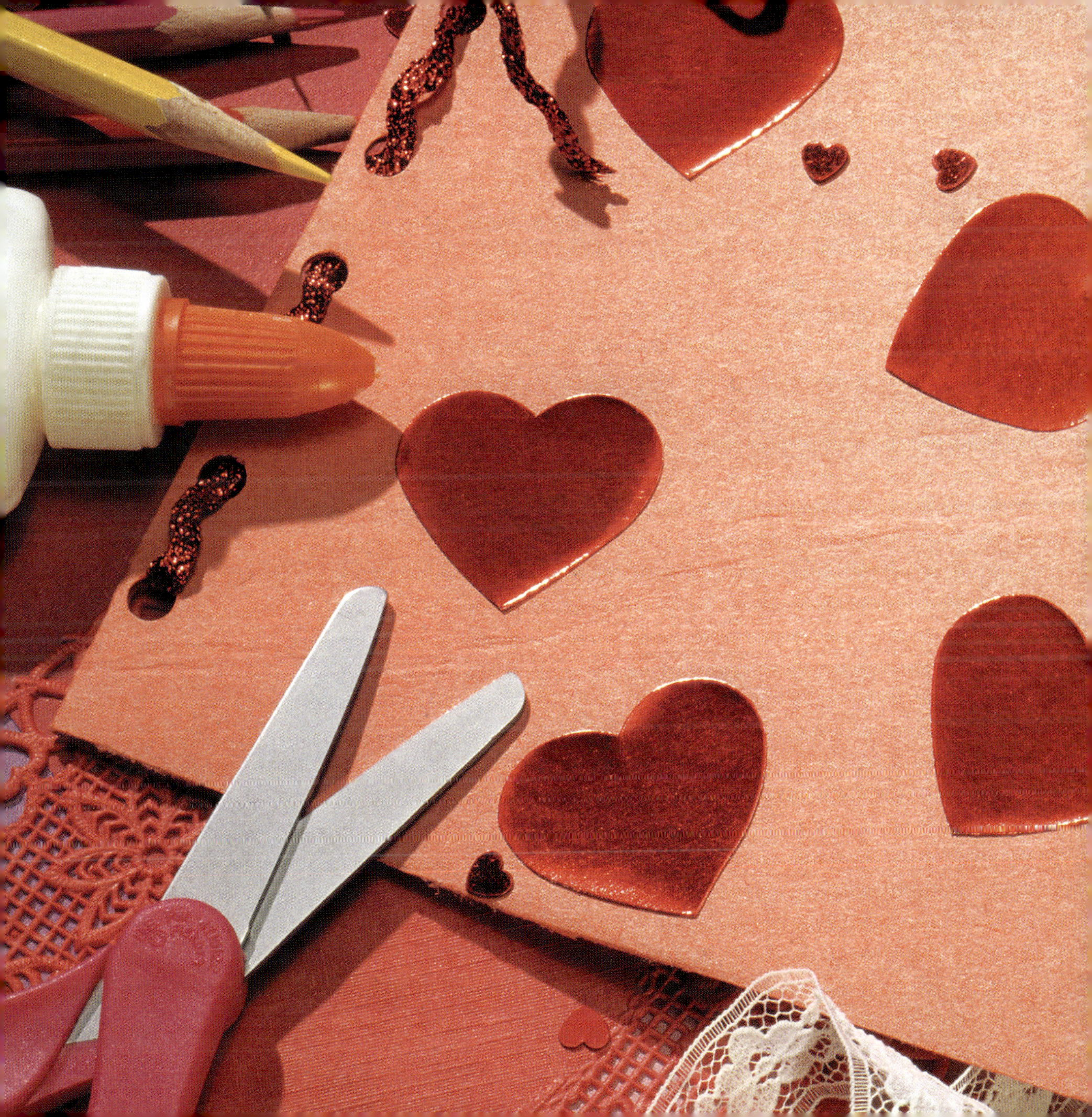

May
This bow of white
Which gives delight,
And which I send you
A token be of Love devine
Oh, will't thou be
My Valentine.

OLD-FASHIONED VALENTINES

The first large numbers of paper valentines were made in the early 1800s in England. Americans began the practice by the mid-1800s.

Many of the early valentines were painted by hand. Some were decorated with feathers, seashells, dried flowers, and make-believe jewelry. Even today valentine cards are still a popular way of showing love.

Old valentines were fancy and made by hand.

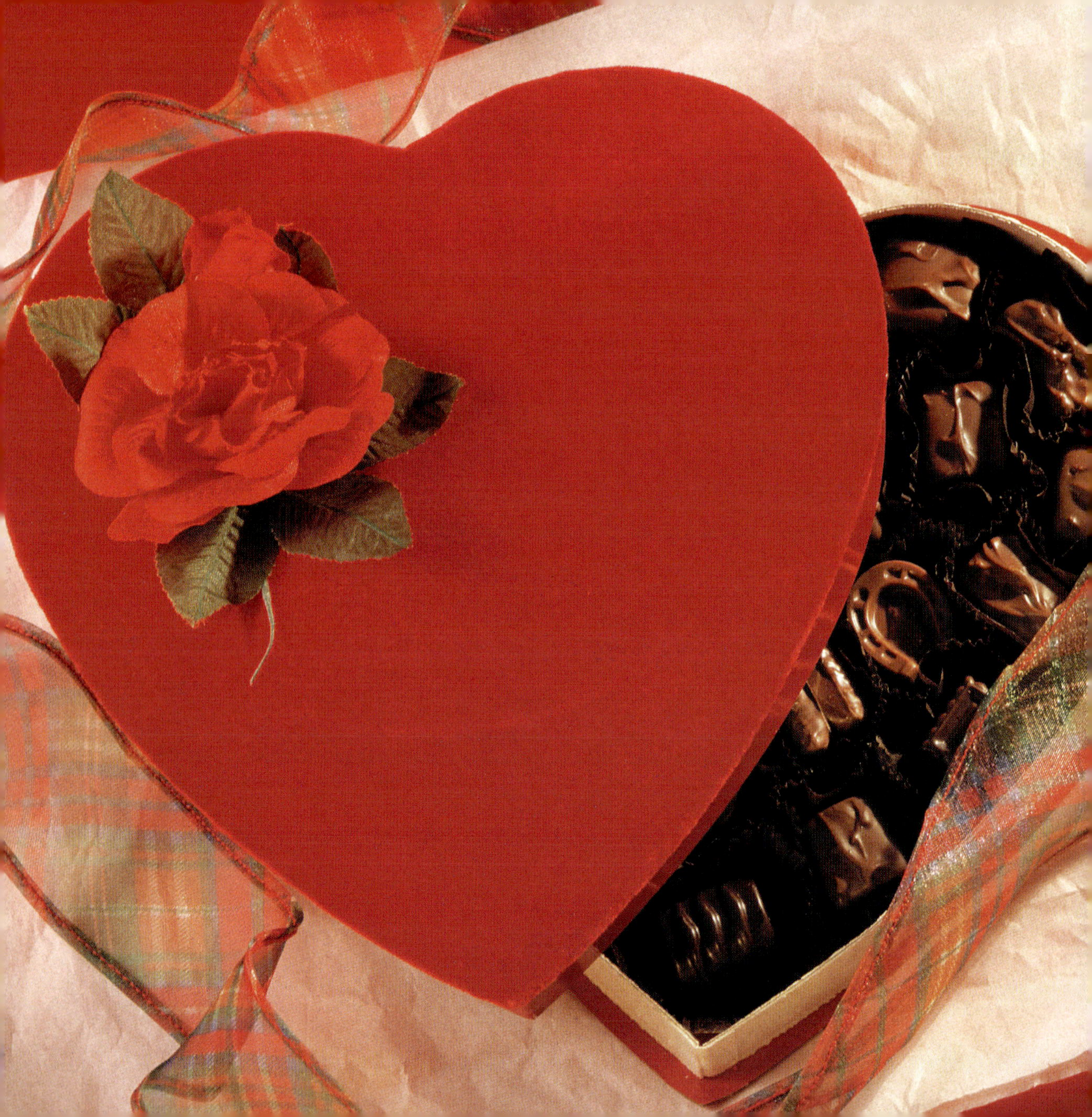

VALENTINE SYMBOLS

People often decorate classrooms, stores, and restaurants with valentine **symbols** as February 14 comes closer. Symbols are those things that stand for something else. Around Valentine's Day, the best known symbol is a heart shape. Many valentine cards, candies, gift boxes, cookies, and pieces of jewelry are heart-shaped.

A candy box in the shape of a heart is a favorite way to send Valentine's Day greetings.

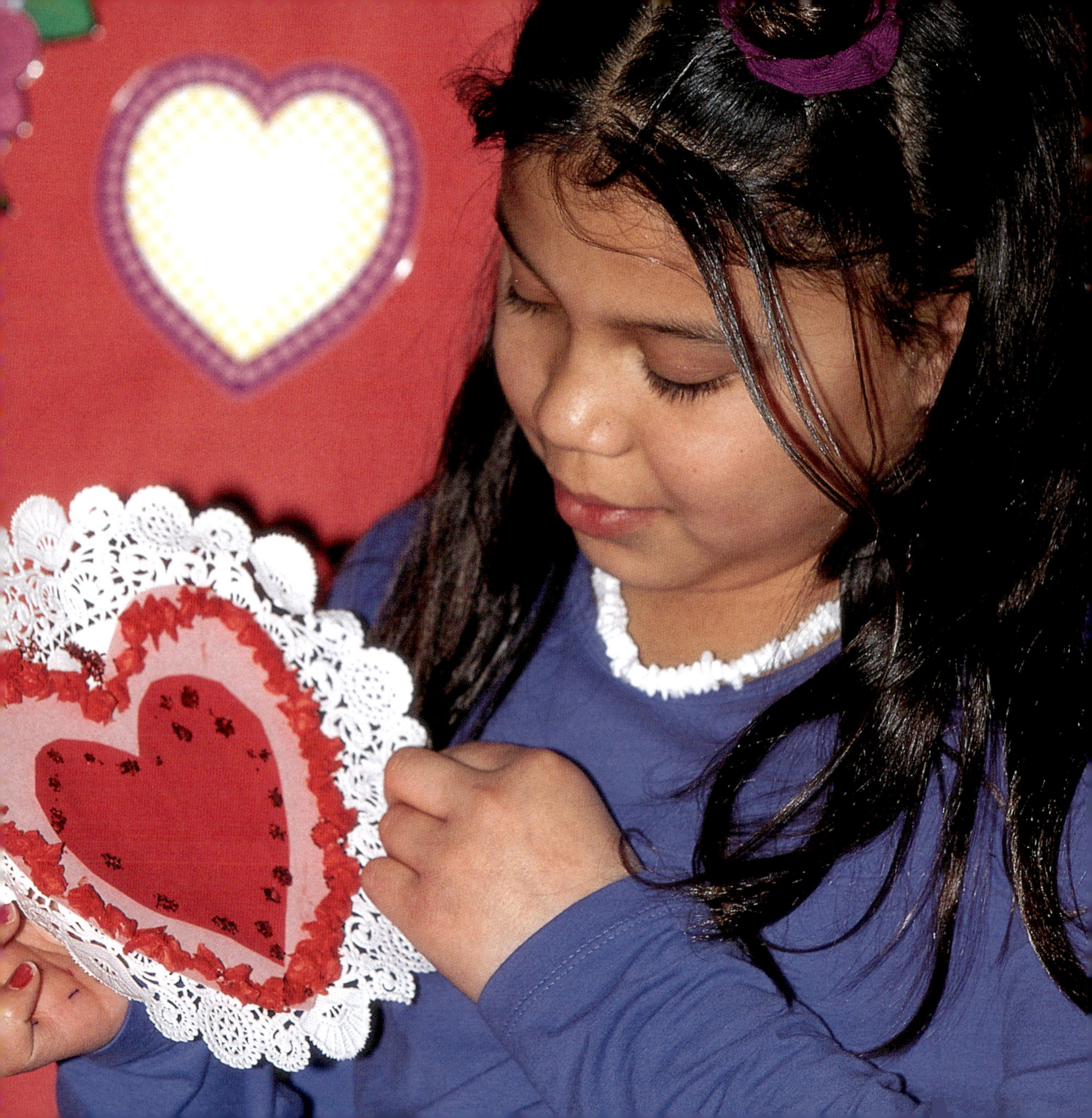

RED AND WHITE

Most Valentine's Day hearts are red, like many other symbols of this day. Red symbolizes warm feelings.

Another symbol of the day is fancy white lace. White is a symbol of purity. Many valentine cards have a border of paper lace.

White lace is a popular Valentine's Day symbol.

ROSES ARE RED

Flowers are another Valentine's Day symbol. Flowers are symbols of **affection**. Pictures of flowers appear on valentine cards and gifts. People often give flowers to those they love.

The rose is the best known of Valentine's Day flowers. Red roses, in fact, are symbols of love!

White doves are Valentine's Day symbols, too. Doves are symbols of peace and love. The birds are usually shown as a pair, each looking fondly at the other.

People often give red roses on Valentine's Day.

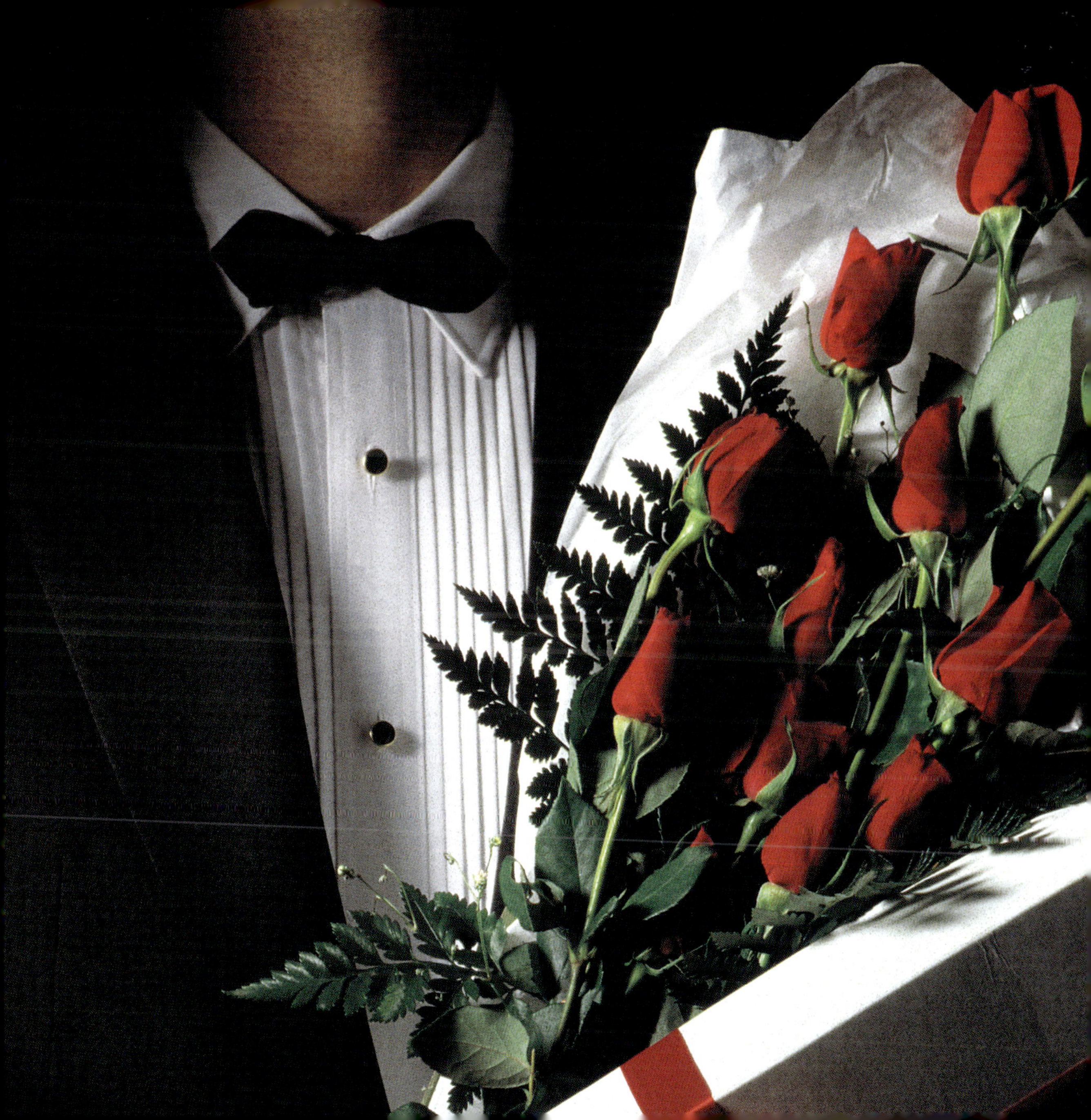

CUPID

After the heart shape, **Cupid** is the best known of Valentine's Day symbols. Cupid looks like a plump child. He is usually shown with darts or a bow and arrows.

Cupid's arrows are not meant to harm. They are arrows of love. The old tale says that if Cupid shoots an arrow into your heart, you will fall helplessly in love. People are said to be "playing Cupid" when they try to match a boy and girl **romantically**.

Cupid is supposed to help young people fall in love.

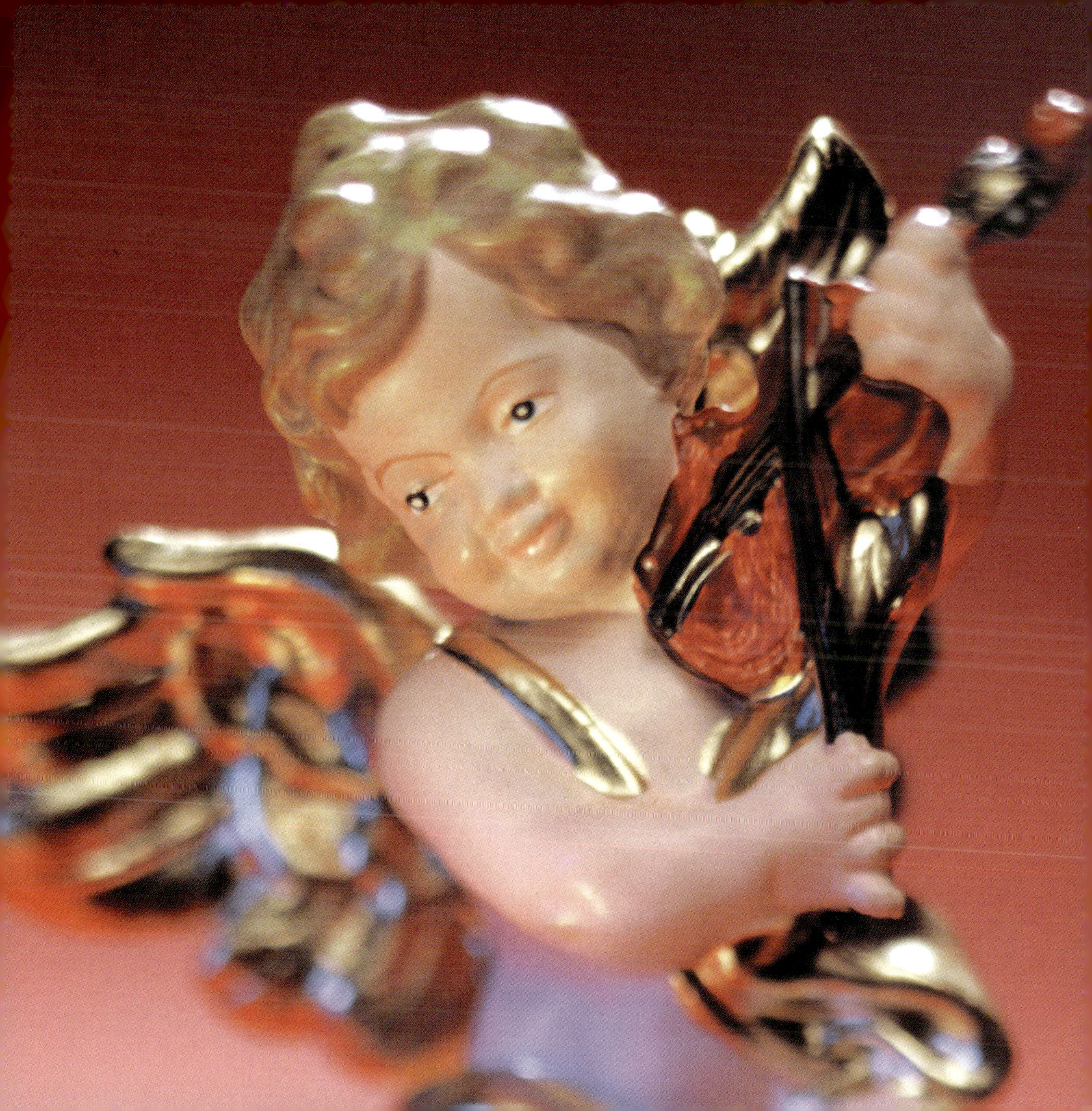

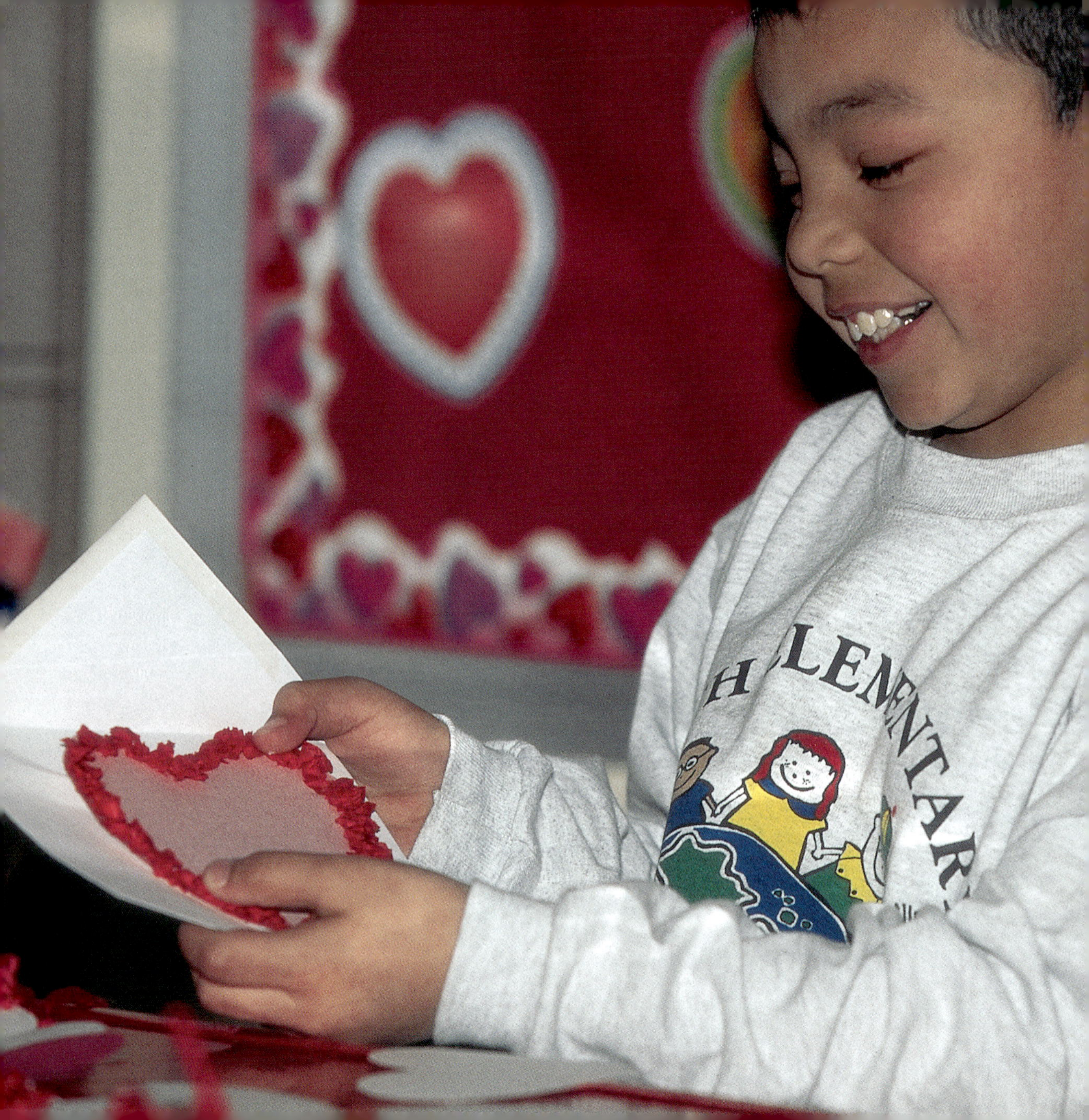

ROMANS AND GREEKS

Cupid was around long before Valentine's Day. The **ancient** Romans and Greeks worshipped several gods and goddesses. In the Roman world, Cupid was the son of Venus. She was the goddess of love and beauty. In the world of Greek gods, Cupid was known as **Eros**.

A valentine about to be sent always brings a smile.

THE FIRST VALENTINE'S DAYS

We know how and when most of our holidays and other special days began. No one is sure how Valentine's Day began, but there are several ideas.

For example, the early Christian Church in Rome had at least two saints named Valentine. The first Valentine was a special friend to children. When he was put in prison for his Christian beliefs, children passed loving notes through the jail bars to him. **Legend** says he was put to death by the government on February 14 in the year 269.

People of all ages enjoy making valentines.

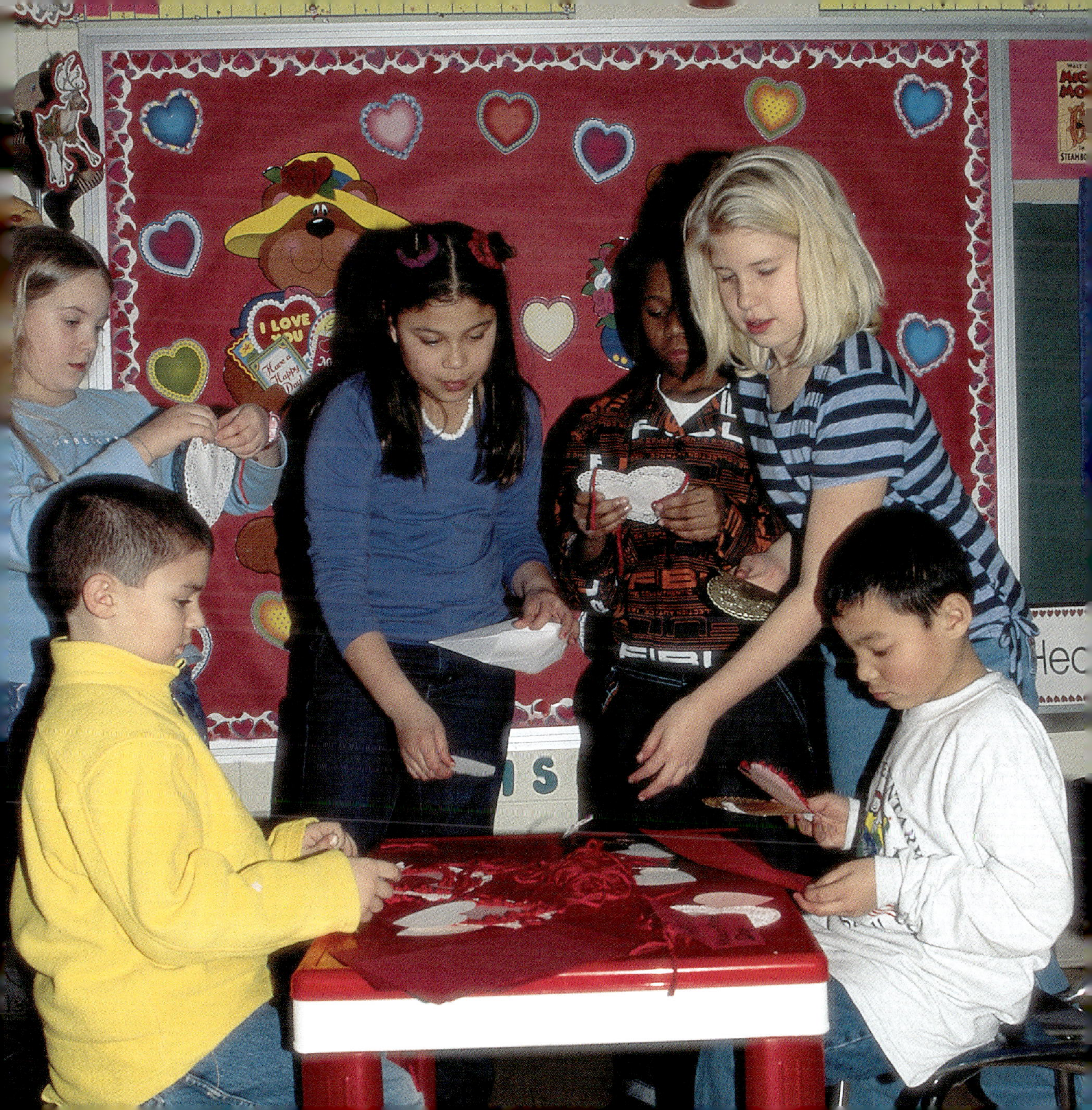
I LOVE YOU
Have a Happy Day!

EARLY VALENTINE'S DAYS

The second Valentine was a priest who secretly married young men to their sweethearts. He did so even though the Roman ruler had kept young men from getting married. The ruler thought that men without wives would be better soldiers.

The English may have celebrated Valentine's Day as far back as the 1400s. They linked Valentine's Day to a day in February when, in legend, birds chose their mates.

GLOSSARY

affection (uh FECK shun) — a warm feeling toward someone

ancient (AIN shunt) — very old; from olden times

Cupid (KEW pud) — a Roman Valentine's Day symbol, usually shown with bows and arrows

Eros (EAR oss) — the Greek name for Cupid

fondness (FAWNED ness) — affection, love

legend (LEDGE und) — an old tale that may not be entirely true but that has been repeated often over the years

romantically (roh MAN tick lee) — having to do with a loving relationship between two unrelated people

symbols (СIM bulz) — objects that stand for something else

INDEX

cards   6, 13, 14
Cupid   16
doves   14
February 14   5, 11, 20
flowers   14
hearts   13

lace   13
love   9, 14, 16
rose   14
Saint Valentine   20
symbols   11, 13, 14, 16
valentines   6, 9

Further Reading

Bulla, Clyde Robert. *The Story of Valentine's Day*. Harper Collins, 1999
Roop, Connie. *Let's Celebrate Valentine's Day*. Millbrook Press, 1999

Websites To Visit

http://www.kidsdomain.com/holiday/val/

About The Author

Jason Cooper has written several children's books about a variety of topics for Rourke Publishing, including recent series *China Discovery* and *American Landmarks*. Cooper travels widely to gather information for his books. Two of his favorite travel destinations are Alaska and the Far East.